MW00900368

Express Yourself!

Cover illustration by Tommy Stubbs and Jim Durk
Interior illustrations by Jim Durk

A GOLDEN BOOK · NEW YORK
Thomas the Tank Engine & Friends™

CREATED BY BRITT ALLCROFT

Based on The Railway Series by The Reverend W Awdry.
© 2011 Gullane (Thomas) LLC.
Thomas the Tank Engine & Friends and Thomas & Friends are trademarks of Gullane (Thomas) Limited.
HIT and the HIT Entertainment logo are trademarks of HIT Entertainment Limited.
All rights reserved. Published in the United States by Golden Books, an imprint of Random House Children's Books, a division
of Random House, Inc., 1745 Broadway, New York, NY 10019, and in Canada by Random House of Canada Limited, Toronto.
Golden Books, A Golden Book, and the G colophon are registered trademarks of Random House, Inc.
ISBN: 978-0-375-86603-6
www.randomhouse.com/kids
www.thomasandfriends.com
Printed in the United States of America
10 9 8 7 6 5 4 3 2

HiT entertainment

"Hello! I'm Thomas. What's your name?
Will you write it here?"

"The pictures in this book need to be finished.
Are you ready to help?"

Will you add some windows to Annie?

Don't forget Clarabel's windows.

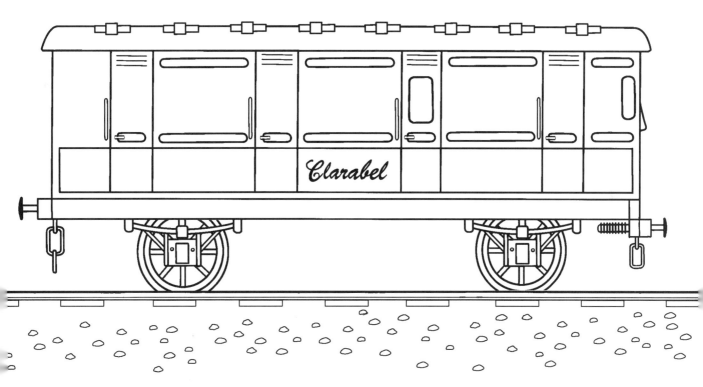

Will you draw a number 1 on Thomas' side?

Let's buy two tickets for a ride with Thomas.
Will you add some money to the counter?

"What a beautiful day," says Sir Topham Hatt. Will you draw a sun in the sky?

Where is Sir Topham Hatt's hat? Will you finish it for him?

Where is Thomas' driver?

Percy is a bright green engine. Will you draw something else that is green?

Will you draw a 6 on Percy's side?

Will you draw another wheel for Percy?

Draw some steam puffing out of Percy's funnel.

Percy wants to know what time it is.

Using this page as a model, can you draw Percy's face on the next page?

Will you draw a 5 on James' side?

James is a shiny red engine. Will you draw something else that is red?

James likes balloons. Will you draw some for him?

Draw some tracks so James can get to Knapford Station.

James is being Really Useful.
What is he delivering?

It's time to give James some coal, but where is the shovel?

Fill Mavis' hopper with rocks.

Will you draw a 3 on Henry's tender?

Elizabeth is making a delivery. Will you load her full of apples?

Elizabeth needs a road that will lead to Cranky. Can you draw one?

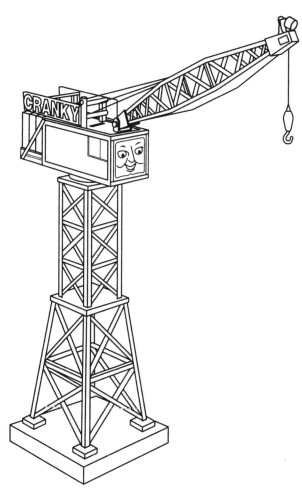

What is Cranky loading into the Troublesome Truck?

What is Harold carrying?

Will you draw a 2 on Edward's tender?

Harvey's name is missing! Will you write it on his side?

Alfie is hard at work. Help him by drawing the hole he is digging.

Jeremy the Jet Plane is flying high. Draw him some clouds.

Thomas is lost at sea! Will you draw water around him?

Thomas needs to haul a shipment of logs. Will you draw a stack of logs on this car for him?

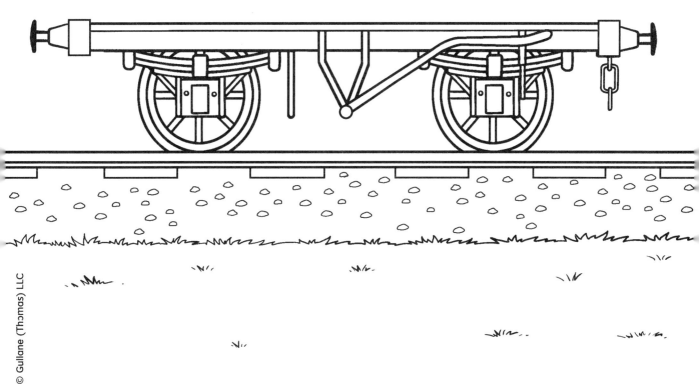

On Misty Island, Ol' Weezy likes throwing logs more than stacking them. Draw **some** logs in the air.

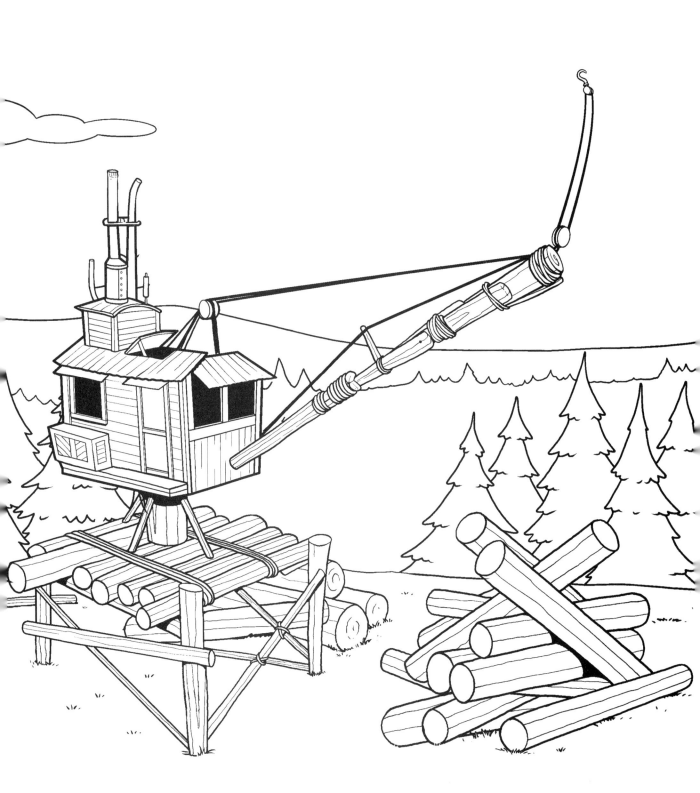

Where are Whiff's glasses? Will you draw them on him?

Emily is a Really Useful Engine. What is she pulling?

Will you draw a big X so Harold knows where to land?

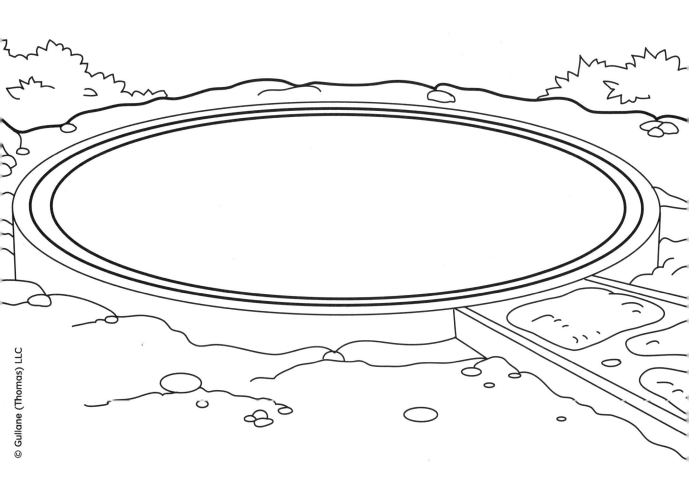

Time to pick up the mail. Will you draw some mailbags for Percy to deliver?

Will you draw a big pile of coal for Salty?

Salty has to deliver three barrels. Will you draw the third one for him?

Will you draw cars for Thomas, James, and Percy to pull?

After all this work, Thomas needs water.
Will you draw some water for him?

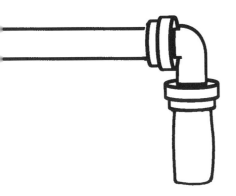

Draw some steam puffing out of Thomas' funnel.

Draw your very own Really Useful Engine here.

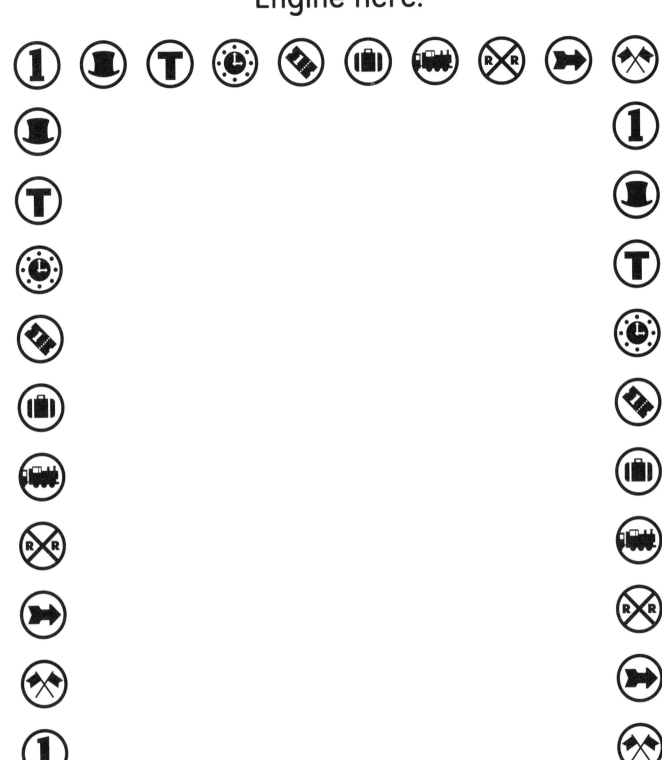

Oh, no! It's raining. How many raindrops can you draw in the sky?

Connect the dots to make an umbrella for Sir Topham Hatt.

2

3

4

5

1

12

13

11

10

9

8

7

6

Will you add some lightning to the sky?

Achoo! Percy is sneezing. Will you draw some steam puffing from his funnel?

Thomas loves splashing through puddles.
Will you draw some for him?

How many leaves can you draw on the ground?

Sir Topham Hatt thinks this station needs a new door. Will you draw one?

The man is going to paint the station.
Will you draw another can
of paint for him?

Will you help the woman make the station pretty? Draw some flowers in the window boxes.

This luggage cart needs wheels.
Will you draw some?

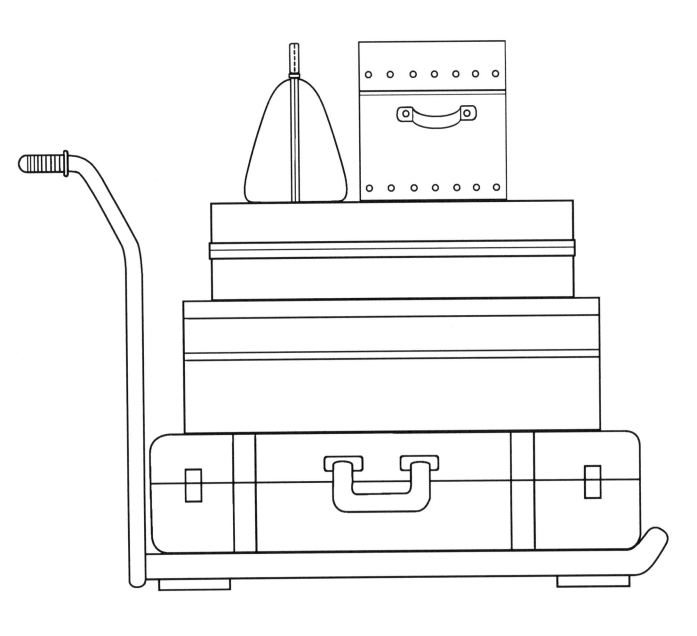

Connect the dots to help the Station Master finish hanging the banners.

This is the most beautiful station on Sodor! Will you add some balloons to celebrate?

Will you finish the sign?

Which engine is pulling into the station?

Sir Topham Hatt is ready for a trip, but where is his suitcase?

James likes the flowers in the country.
Will you draw some more for him?

Watch out for the bees, James!
Will you add some bees to the scene?

Henry loves the forest. Will you draw some tall trees behind him?

Will you draw some water and fishy friends for Bulstrode?

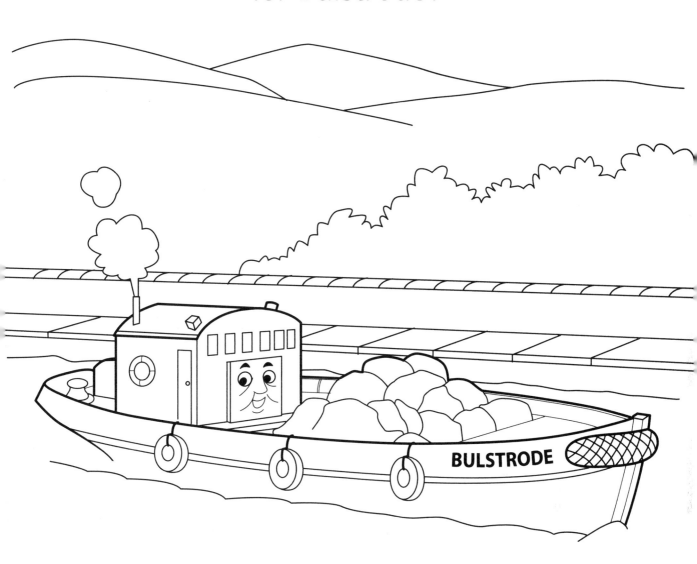

BULSTRODE

James needs a bridge to cross.

Will you draw the rest of Rolf's Castle?

Add some colorful flags to the castle.

Arf! Arf! A little dog wants to say hello to Thomas. Will you draw him?

Will you help the artist paint a picture of something on Sodor?

Bertie loves the beach. Make a sand castle for him.

Percy likes butterflies. Will you draw a few more for him?

Who's in the nest?

Will you draw some birds to keep Harold company?

Who is Spencer racing?

Draw some steam puffing out of
Rosie's funnel.

Draw a boat racing Thomas to the Docks.

Make sure the signal arm is raised so Bertie can cross the tracks.

Percy thinks it's a perfect day for a picnic. Will you draw a blanket for the children to sit on?

Thomas wants to see a kite flying high in the sky. Will you draw it?

Will you draw some fish in the water?

What did the boy catch?

Will you draw a leash for the dog?

This crossing needs a stop sign. Will you draw one for Molly and Elizabeth?

Add a circle to finish the traffic light. Then color it to make Bertie stop.

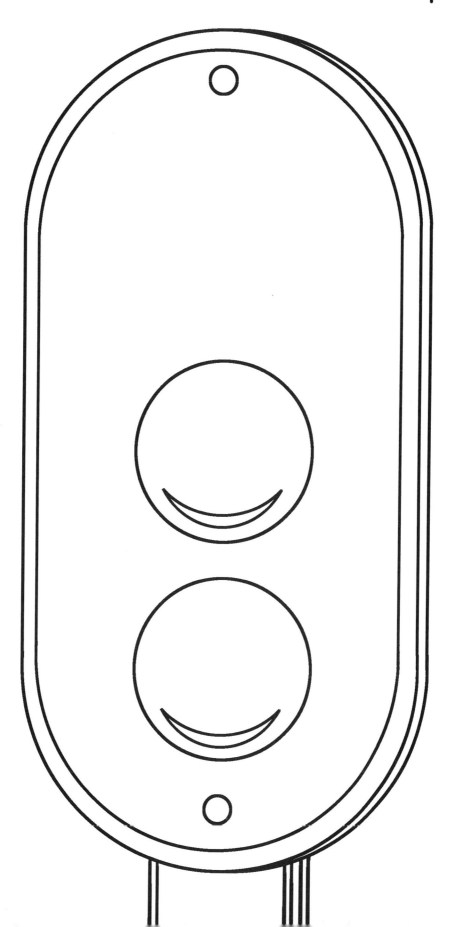

Will you finish the sign?

Who is on the bridge waving to James?

Draw tracks so Percy can steam down the hill.

Thomas is following the hot-air balloon. Will you finish it?

Will you draw some apples in the trees behind Oliver?

Who is Harvey talking to?

Will you draw a 4 on Gordon's tender?

Will you draw a tunnel for James?

Watch out, Bertie! There's something in the road!

Bertie is waiting for his friends to cross the street. Will you draw some more baby ducks?

Will you draw a funny scarecrow waving at Percy?

Thomas is climbing higher and higher.
Will you draw some mountains?

Thomas and Percy are looking for a rainbow.
Will you draw one for them?

The circus is coming to town!
Will you draw a big tent?

Thomas wants to help bring the animals to the circus! Will you draw an elephant in Thomas' car?

Will you draw some balls for the clown to juggle?

Percy loves to watch the clowns. What is the clown balancing on?

Will you draw a friend for this monkey?

Will you draw balloons for the boy at the circus?

Jack needs some tires.

What is Kevin lifting?

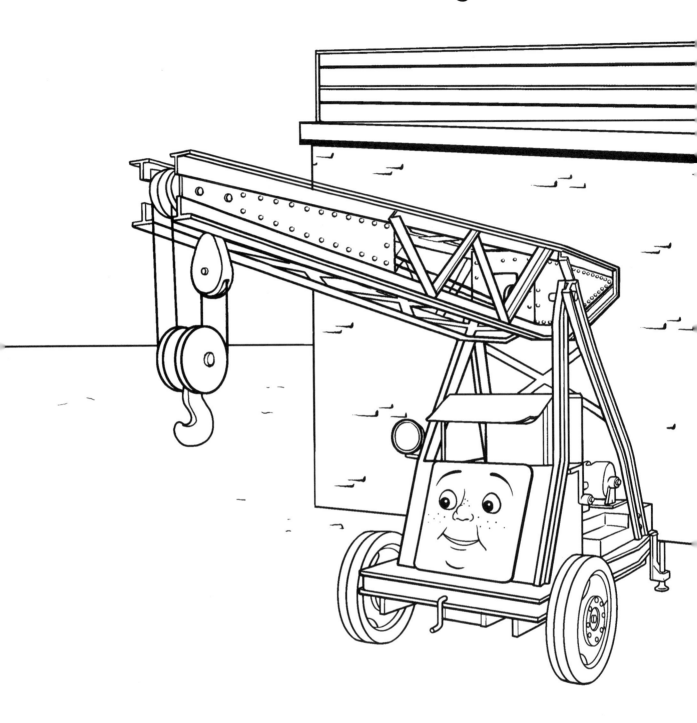

Safety first!
Will you finish the cones for Victor?

Victor needs two more drums of oil for the Sodor Steamworks. Will you draw them?

There are lots of repairs to do at the Sodor Steamworks. Can you draw two more wheels?

Thomas needs some new paint. Will you trace the dashed lines to help him?

It looks like Percy needs a new funnel.

Draw two new wheels for James.

Will you draw some tools for this toolbox?

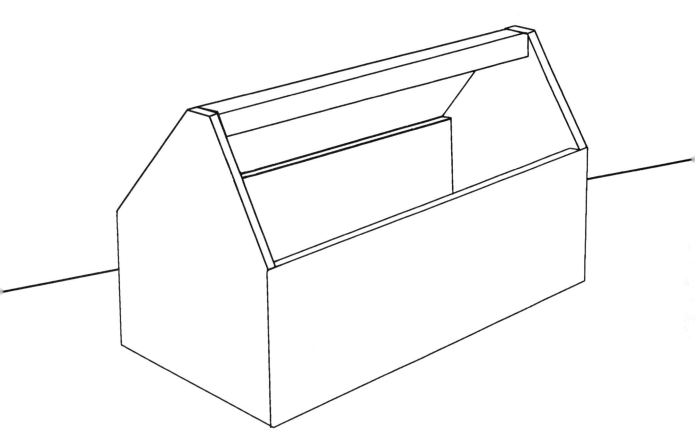

Oh, no! The track is broken.
Can you repair it?

Is it safe to cross?
Help Thomas make sure the signal is raised.

Draw two more wheels for Thomas.

Will you finish the sign?

Using this page as a model, can you draw Thomas' face on the next page?

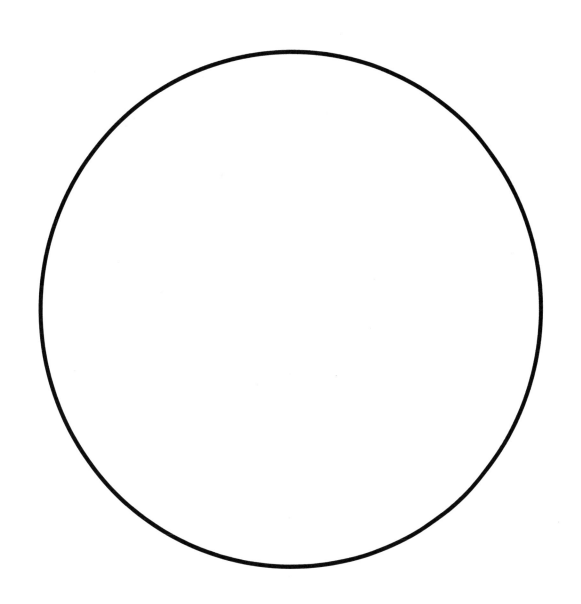

Will you draw a cake
for Thomas' birthday party?

These cards for Thomas need stamps.

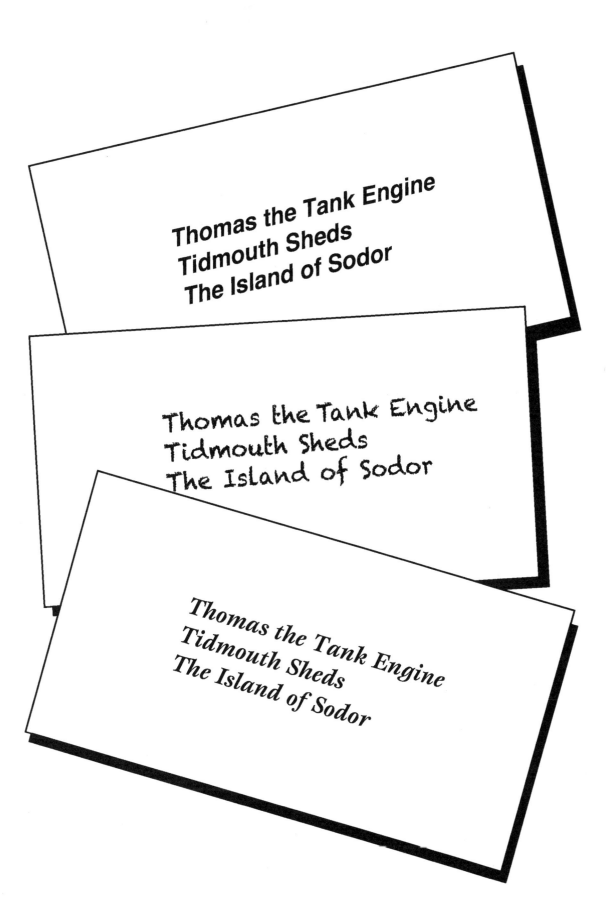

Thomas the Tank Engine
Tidmouth Sheds
The Island of Sodor

Thomas the Tank Engine
Tidmouth Sheds
The Island of Sodor

Thomas the Tank Engine
Tidmouth Sheds
The Island of Sodor

Will you draw another hat for Thomas' birthday party?

Will you decorate the birthday banner for Thomas' party?

Who is Gordon speaking to?

Draw your best friend with Percy.

It's nighttime on the Island of Sodor. Will you draw a moon in the sky?

Will you finish the roof on Tidmouth Sheds?

It's been a busy day. Now it's time to rest.
Draw some stars in the night sky.